A
STONE
SAT STILL

BRENDAN WENZEL

chronicle books · san francisco

A stone sat still
with the water, grass, and dirt

and it was as it was
where it was in the world.

And the stone was dark

and the stone was bright

and the stone was loud

and the stone was quiet

and it sat where it sat
with the water, grass, and dirt

and it was as it was
where it was in the world.

And the stone was rough

and the stone was smooth

and the stone was green

red

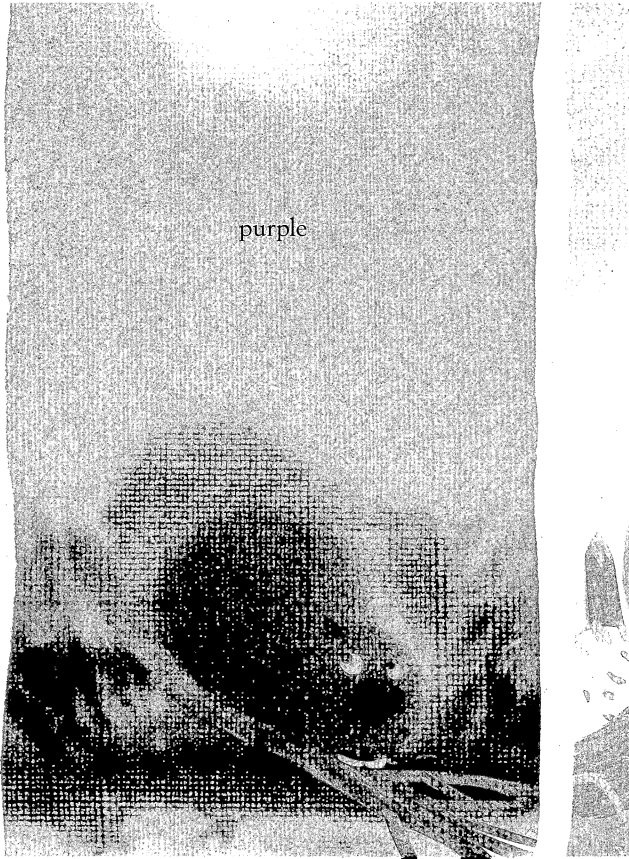

purple

and blue.

And the stone was a pebble

and the stone was a hill

and the stone was a feel

and the stone was a smell

and it sat where it sat
with the water, grass, and dirt

and it was as it was
where it was in the world.

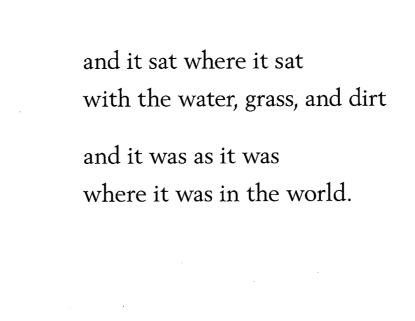

And the stone was the wild

and the stone was a home

and the stone was a kitchen

and the stone was a throne.

And the stone was a marker

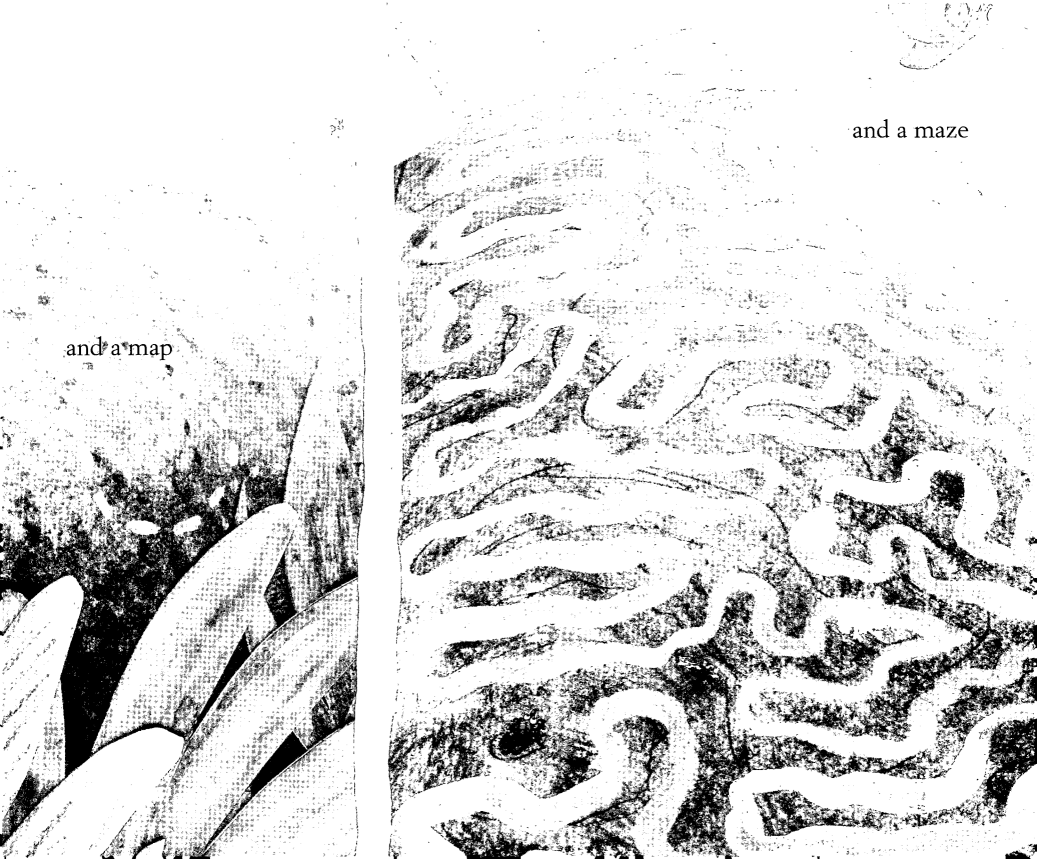

and a maze

and a map

a danger

a haven

a story

a stage.

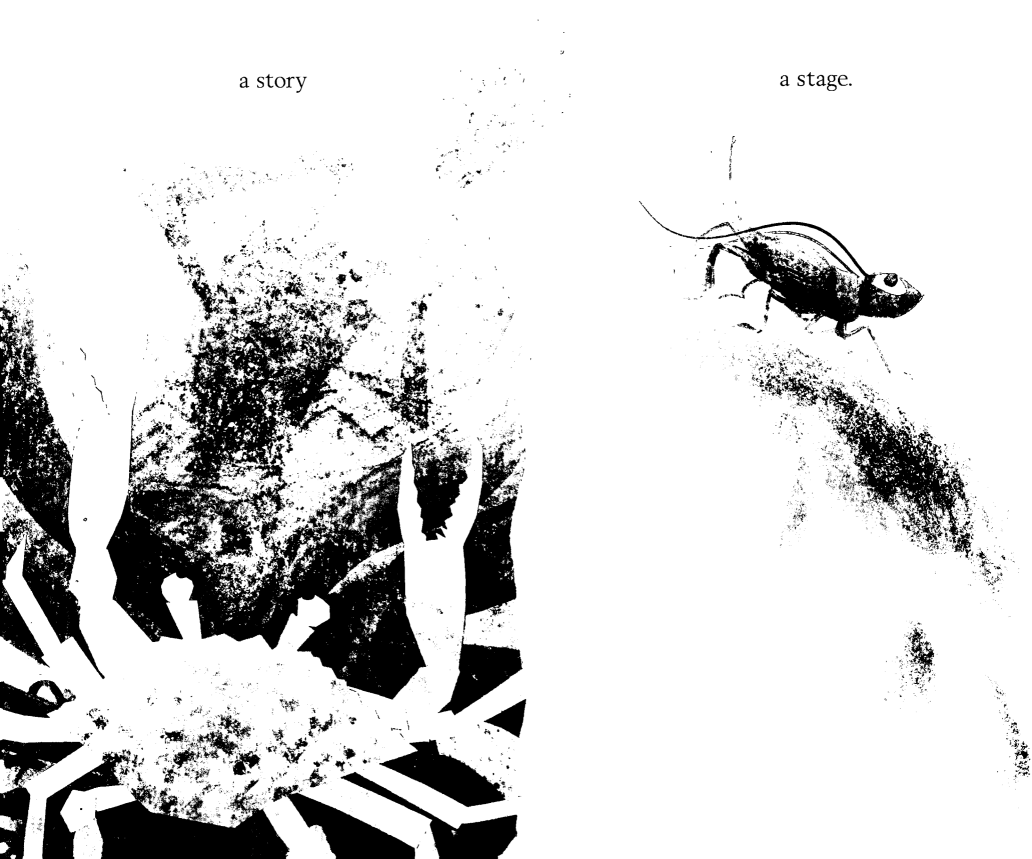

And the stone was a blink

and the stone was an age.

And the stone was an island

and the stone was a wave

and the stone was a memory

and the stone was always.

Have you ever known such a place?

Where with water, grass, and dirt

a stone sits still in the world.

For Ophelia and Kallisti—B.W.

Library of Congress Cataloging-in-Publication Data

Names: Wenzel, Brendan, author, illustrator.
Title: A stone sat still / Brendan Wenzel.
Description: San Francisco, California : Chronicle Books LLC,
[2019] |
    Summary: Told in rhyming verse, a stone is considered
    from a variety of environmental and emotional perspectives,
    as it sits where it is, surrounded by grass, dirt, and water,
    an unchanging certainty in the world.
Identifiers: LCCN 2018048432 | ISBN 9781452173184
    (hardcover)
Subjects: LCSH: Stone—Juvenile fiction. | Perception—Juvenile
    fiction .| Nature (Aesthetics)—Juvenile fiction. | Stories in rhyme. |
    CYAC: Stories in rhyme. | Rocks—Fiction. | Perception—
    Fiction. | Nature—Fiction. | LCGFT: Stories in rhyme.
Classification: LCC PZ8.3.W4653 St 2019 |
    DDC [E]—dc23 LC record available at
    https://lccn.loc.gov/2018048432

Manufactured in China.

Design by Jennifer Tolo Pierce.
Typeset in Berling.
The illustrations in this book were rendered in a variety
of media, including cut paper, colored pencil, oil pastels,
marker, and the computer.

10 9 8 7 6 5 4 3 2 1

Chronicle Books LLC
680 Second Street
San Francisco, California 94107

Chronicle Books—we see things differently. Become part
of our community at www.chroniclekids.com.